THE CREEPING
BOOKENDS

BY MICHAEL DAHL
ILLUSTRATED BY BRADFORD KENDALL

Librarian Reviewer
Laurie K. Holland
Media Specialist (National Board Certified), Edina, MN
MA in Elementary Education, Minnesota State University, Mankato

Reading Consultant
Elizabeth Stedem
Educator/Consultant, Colorado Springs, CO
MA in Elementary Education, University of Denver, CO

STONE ARCH BOOKS
Minneapolis   San Diego

Zone Books are published by Stone Arch Books,
151 Good Counsel Drive, P.O. Box 669,
Mankato, Minnesota 56002.
www.stonearchbooks.com

Library of Congress Cataloging-in-Publication Data
Dahl, Michael.
  The Creeping Bookends / by Michael Dahl; illustrated by
Bradford Kendall.
    p. cm. — (Zone books — Library of Doom)
    ISBN 978-1-4342-0486-8 (library binding)
    ISBN 978-1-4342-0546-9 (paperback)
    [1. Books and reading—Fiction. 2. Librarians—Fiction.
3. Fantasy.] I. Kendall, Bradford, ill. II. Title.
PZ7.D15134Cre 2008
[Fic]—dc22   2007032221

Summary: One evening, a young boy is accidentally locked inside
a library. Suddenly, a pair of lizard bookends come alive! The boy
watches as the ravenous reptiles gobble up stacks of books. Will
the Librarian arrive before the boy becomes their next meal?

Creative Director: Heather Kindseth
Senior Designer for Cover and Interior: Kay Fraser
Graphic Designer: Brann Garvey

1 2 3 4 5 6 12 11 10 09 08 07

Printed in the United States of America.

TABLE OF CONTENTS

Chapter One

Locked In. 5

Chapter Two

A Flash of Light 10

Chapter Three

Attack of the Bookends. 15

Chapter Four

Twisting Tails 21

Chapter Five

Lightning and Dust 28

The Library of Doom is the world's largest collection of strange and dangerous books. The Librarian's duty is to keep the books from falling into the hands of those who would use them for evil purposes.

CHAPTER 1

Lightning flashes above an old library in a small town.

Wind rattles the windows and shakes the doors.

Rain beats against the roof.

Inside, an ancient clock strikes ten o'clock.

The quiet visitors gather up their books and head toward the doors.

An old library worker **turns off the lights.**

She leaves the building and locks the door behind her.

A **dark shape** moves behind one of the shelves.

It's a **young boy.**

When everyone
else left, he
was reading
behind a tall
bookshelf.

Now he is locked
inside the library.

The boy sees a pale
green glow.

CHAPTER 2

A FLASH OF LIGHT

The glow comes from a large fireplace across the room.

Above the fireplace sits a thick book held in place by **two strange bookends.**

The book is glowing.

But the boy isn't looking at the book. He is staring at the |bookends| .

The bookends are shaped like **monsters** with wide **angry** mouths and `lizard tails.`

Their eyes are shut. They look as if they are <u>sleeping</u>.

Another streak of lightning **flashes** through the windows.

The bright light blinds the boy for an instant.

Then the boy looks up at the
fireplace.

One of the bookends is blinking.
The other bookend snaps its tail.

They are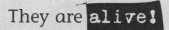

❰ CHAPTER 3 ❱

ATTACK OF THE BOOKENDS

The bookends slither down the fireplace.

The **strange creatures** climb up the library bookshelves.

At each shelf they stop to devour books.

They crunch and chew their way through the paper and covers.

"Stop!" yells the boy. "You shouldn't do that!"

The **hungry** bookends ignore him.

They rip the books apart with their fearsome jaws.

The boy reaches out and grabs the **tail** of one of the bookends.

He pulls hard.

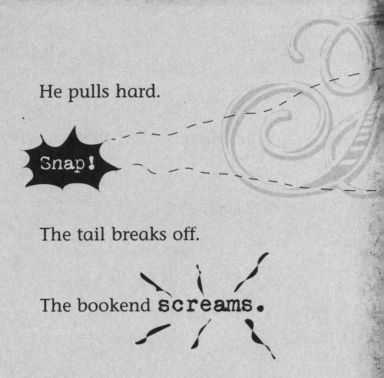

Snap!

The tail breaks off.

The bookend **screams.**

The creature quickly grows a new tail.

The boy looks down at the old tail in his hand.

He drops it onto the floor.

The tail squirms and slithers.

Then it begins to grow.

As the boy stares at the lizard tail,
it turns into a new creature.

CHAPTER 4

TWISTING TAILS

Now there are three hungry bookends.

The lizards gaze down at the boy from the bookshelves.

They **hiss** and **bite** each other.

They **chew** each other's **tails off.**

As each new tail hits the floor, it grows into a **new `lizard`.**

Soon, the library is full of
`swarming, screaming,`
`slithering` bookend lizards.

The boy **climbs** up on the fireplace
to escape the rushing swarm.

The lizards **bite** and **gulp** the rest
of the library books.

In minutes all the books have been eaten, but the bookends are **still hungry.**

Where will they find more food?

One by one the creatures turn to <u>stare</u> at the frightened boy.

The bookends lick their lizard lips.

(CHAPTER 5)

LIGHTNING AND DUST

Boom!

A bolt of `lightning` breaks one of the windows!

The boy blinks his eyes. A strange man stands in the middle of the library.

"You're **the Librarian**,"
says the boy. "I've read stories
about you."

"Do you believe everything you
read?" asks the Librarian.

"Yes," says the boy.

The Librarian **smiles**. "Good," he says.

The Librarian points at the
`glowing book` on top of the
fireplace.

"I've come for my book," he says.

A stream of lightning shoots from
his fingers.

The lightning hits the glowing
book. The blaze shines like a
`thousand suns.`

The boy **hides** his face with his hands.

When the boy looks up, the book is gone.

All the lizard bookends have been destroyed. Now they are only piles of dust.

The Librarian is gone.

The boy sees that the door to the library is no longer locked.

The storm has stopped.

Now he can **go** home.

~ **THE END** ~

A PAGE FROM THE LIBRARY OF DOOM

LIZARD TAILS

Lizards may seem like gross creatures, but some animals, such as eagles and snakes, enjoy eating them for lunch! So lizards have developed a tricky way to escape from danger. They shed their tails.

When a lizard is fleeing a large predator, the predator may grab or bite onto the lizard's tail. The tail snaps off, allowing the lizard to run to safety. This ability to lose one's tail is called **tail shedding**.

Some lizard tails wiggle and squirm after they snap off. The moving tail helps to distract the lizard's enemy. Some **gecko** tails can wiggle for as long as five minutes!

A **skink** is a lizard that spends much of its time in the water. It uses its tail to paddle. If it sheds its tail, though, it can't swim.

Most tails grow back. Smaller lizards grow them back in a month. But it can take a year for a larger lizard, like an iguana, to regrow its long tail. Only the soft parts of the tail grow back. The tailbone does not.

Lizards also use their tails to store energy and fat. If food is hard to come by, lizards without tails will starve faster than lizards with tails.

Lizards are not the only creatures that can lose a body part to escape from danger. Crabs, spiders, and some starfish do the same thing with their legs!

ABOUT THE AUTHOR

Michael Dahl is the author of more than 100 books for children and young adults. He has twice won the AEP Distinguished Achievement Award for his nonfiction. His Finnegan Zwake mystery series was chosen by the Agatha Awards to be among the five best mystery books for children in 2002 and 2003. He collects books on poison and graveyards, and lives in a haunted house in Minneapolis, Minnesota.

ABOUT THE ILLUSTRATOR

Bradford Kendall has enjoyed drawing for as long as he can remember. As a boy, he loved to read comic books and watch old monster movies. He graduated from the Rhode Island School of Design with a BFA in Illustration. He has owned his own commercial art business since 1983, and lives in Providence, Rhode Island, with his wife, Leigh, and their two children Lily and Stephen. They also have a cat named Hansel and a dog named Gretel. Sometimes, they all sit together to watch an old monster movie.

GLOSSARY

ancient (AYN-shuhnt)—something that is very, very old

blaze (BLAYZ)—a large, hot fire

bookends (BOOK-endz)—supports placed at each end of a row of books to hold them up

destroyed (di-STROYD)—completely ruined

devour (di-VOWER)—to eat up something quickly

fearsome (FEER-suhm)—extremely scary or frightening

slither (SLITH-ur)—to slip or slide around like a snake

swarm (SWORM)—a group of things, like insects or lizards, that gather or move together

DISCUSSION QUESTIONS

1. What made the creeping bookends come to life? Was it the lightning? Was it the strange glowing book? Was it something else? Explain.

2. The Librarian asks the young boy, "Do you believe everything you read?" How would you answer this question? Explain your answer.

3. What do you think might have happened if the Librarian wouldn't have shown up? Do you believe the boy could have escaped the library alone? Why or why not?

WRITING PROMPTS

1. The setting of a book is where the story takes place. This story happens inside a library. Write your own completely different story with the same setting.

2. Imagine that the creeping bookends attacked your library. How would you get rid of them? How would you save the books? Write about it.

3. Make a list of three things that give you the creeps. Pick one, and write a scary story about it.

INTERNET SITES

The book may be over, but the adventure is just beginning.

Do you want to read more about the subjects or ideas in this book? Want to play cool games or watch videos about the authors who write these books? Then go to **FactHound**. At *www.facthound.com*, you'll be able to do all that, and more. The FactHound website can also send you to other safe Internet sites.

Check it out!